Show and Tell

Show and Tell

by Robert Munsch
illustrations by Michael Martchenko

annick press
toronto • new york • vancouver

Fifteenth printing, July 2007

Annick Press Ltd.

We acknowledge the support of the Canada Council for the Arts, the Ontario Arts Council, and the Government of Canada through the Book Publishing Industry Development Program (BPIDP) for our publishing activities.

Cataloging in Publication Data

Munsch, Robert N., 1945-
Show and tell

(Munsch for kids)
ISBN 1-55037-195-9 (bound) — ISBN 1-55037-197-5 (pbk.)

I. Martchenko, Michael. II. Title. III. Series:
Munsch, Robert N., 1945- . Munsch for kids.

PS8576.U58S48 1991 jC813'.54 C91-093933-0
PZ7.M86Sh 1991

Distributed in Canada by:
Firefly Books Ltd.
66 Leek Crescent
Richmond Hill, ON
L4B 1H1

Published in the U.S.A. by Annick Press (U.S.) Ltd.
Distributed in the U.S.A. by:
Firefly Books (U.S.) Inc.
P.O. Box 1338
Ellicott Station
Buffalo, NY 14205

Printed and bound in China.

visit us at: **www.annickpress.com**

to Ben and Sharon Chia, Guelph, Ont.

Benjamin wanted to take something really neat to school for show and tell, so he decided to take his new baby sister. He went upstairs, picked her up, put her in his knapsack and walked off to school.

But when Ben sat down, his baby sister finally woke up. She was not happy inside the knapsack and started to cry: "WAAA, WAAA, WAAA, WAAA, WAAA."

The teacher looked at him and said, "Benjamin, stop making that noise."

Ben said, "That's not me. It's my baby sister. She's in my knapsack. I brought her for show and tell."

"Yikes!" said the teacher. "You can't keep a baby in a knapsack!" She grabbed Ben's knapsack and opened it up. The baby looked at the teacher and said, "WAAA, WAAA, WAAA, WAAA, WAAA."

“Don’t worry,” said the teacher. “I know how to take care of babies.” She picked it up and rocked it back and forth, back and forth, back and forth.

Unfortunately, the teacher was not the baby’s mother and she didn’t rock quite right. The baby cried even louder: “WAAA, WAAA, WAAA, WAAA, WAAA.”

The principal came running in. He looked at the teacher and said, “Stop making that noise!”

The teacher said, “It’s not me. It’s Sharon, Ben’s new baby sister. He brought her for show and tell. She won’t shut up!”

The principal said, “Ah, don’t worry. I know how to make kids be quiet.” He picked up the baby and yelled, “HEY, YOU! BE QUIET!” The baby did not like that at all. It screamed, really loudly, “WAAA, WAAA, WAAA, WAAA, WAAA.”

The principal said, “What’s the matter with this baby? It must be sick. I’ll call a doctor.”

The doctor came with a big black bag. She looked in the baby's eyes and she looked in the baby's ears and she looked in the baby's mouth. She said, "Ah! Don't worry. I know what to do. This baby needs a needle!"

So the doctor opened her bag, got out a short needle and said, "Naaaah, TOO SMALL."

The doctor opened her bag, got out a longer needle and said, "Naaaah, TOO SMALL."

The doctor opened her bag, got out a really long needle and said, "Naaaah, TOO SMALL."

The doctor reached into her bag, got out an enormous needle and said, "Ahhh, JUST RIGHT."

When the baby saw that enormous needle, it yelled, as loudly as it could, "WAAA, WAAA, WAAA, WAAA, WAAA."

Ben said, "What's the matter with this school? Nobody knows what to do with a baby." He ran down to the principal's office and called his mother on the phone. He said, "HELP, HELP, HELP! You have to come to school right away."

The mother said, "Ben, your little sister is lost! I can't come to school. I have to find her."

"She's not lost," said Ben. "I took her to school in my knapsack."

"Oh, no!" yelled the mother. She ran down the street and into the school. The principal and the teacher and the doctor were standing around the baby, and the baby was yelling, as loudly as possible, "WAAA, WAAA, WAAA, WAAA, WAAA."

The mother picked up the baby
and rocked it back and forth,
back and forth, back and forth.
The baby said, “Ahhhhhhhhh,”
and went to sleep.

"Oh, thank you! Oh, thank you!" said the principal. "That baby was making so much noise, it was just making me feel sick!"

"SICK?" said the doctor. "SICK! Did that man say he was SICK? He must need a needle." So the doctor opened her bag, got out a short needle and said, "Naaaah, TOO SMALL."

The doctor opened her bag, got out a longer needle and said, "Naaaah, TOO SMALL."

The doctor opened her bag, got out a really long needle and said, "Naaaah, TOO SMALL."

The doctor reached into her bag, got out an enormous needle and said, "Ahhh, JUST RIGHT."

The principal looked at that enormous needle and said, "WAAA, WAAA, WAAA, WAAA, WAAA," and ran out the door.

“Now,” said the mother, “it’s time to take this baby home.”

“Right,” said Ben. “You can use my knapsack.”

“What a good idea,” said the mother.

Ben and his mother put the baby into bed.
She went to sleep and didn't cry, not even once.

Ben went back to school carrying some strange things for show and tell.

And he wasn't out of place at all ...

V
W
Z

Other books in the Munsch for Kids series:

The Dark
Mud Puddle
The Paper Bag Princess
The Boy in the Drawer
Jonathan Cleaned Up, Then He Heard a Sound
Murmel Murmel Murmel
Millicent and the Wind
Mortimer
The Fire Station
Angela's Airplane
David's Father
Thomas' Snowsuit
50 Below Zero
I Have to Go!
Moira's Birthday
A Promise is a Promise
Pigs
Something Good
Purple, Green and Yellow
Wait and See
Where is Gah-Ning?
From Far Away
Stephanie's Ponytail
Munschworks: The First Munsch Collection
Munschworks 2: The Second Munsch Treasury
Munschworks 3: The Third Munsch Treasury
Munschworks 4: The Fourth Munsch Treasury
The Munschworks Grand Treasury

Many Munsch titles are available in French and/or Spanish. Please contact your favorite supplier.